DEAD EYE

BY: NICHOLAS THOMAS ZOGRAFOS

PublishAmerica
Baltimore

First printing

Softcover 978-1-4626-3571-9
PUBLISHED BY PUBLISHAMERICA, LLLP
www.publishamerica.com
Baltimore

Printed in the United States of America

Table of Contents

PREFACE

Sniper Team Twelve is an elite sniper team that is made up of two men, whose names are classified, but are known as Dead Eye and his spotter who is called Snowman. When paired together as a team these two men immediately showed signs of being top notch sniper quality. Dead Eye and Snowman amazed their sniper teachers with their abilities on the training field.

Read how these two men put their lives in danger to save others. This book will take one right into the heart of every mission of this elite sniper team. Join Dead Eye and Snowman from the jungles of Vietnam to the winter wasteland of Siberia as they complete missions that will put them through the ultimate test of their skills and abilities.

1: Sniper Team Twelve, The Beginning Of A Legend

Trained as an elite sniper team, Sniper Team Twelve was the best in the business. In a real life training exercise, Dead Eye got off five shots, and got to within ten yards of two former snipers without being spotted; this was something never before done. The sniper team had gone through two years of elite training and now was ready for the field.

Dead Eye's partner was called Snowman because he was from Alaska. These two when teamed up were the best. When on a training exercise together, they completed the task with perfection. Not a lot was known about their backgrounds, simply because they did not talk about it. The one thing everyone did know was that they were the best.

Due to their superior skills Sniper Team Twelve was recommended for duty immediately. The one problem was that there were no missions at this time for the team. They would have to wait. Little did either of them know but the wait would not be long. Neither of them ever talked about going on a mission, but they were eager to get their feet wet. They would get the chance to prove themselves for the first time in a place thousands of miles away.

2: India

While Sniper Team Twelve was at the range a message came from the officer's headquarters. They were to report immediately to General Link's office. The two got into dress uniform quickly and reported to the officer. Once in the office the team was told the reason they were called, they had their first mission. They were told that they were going to the southern part of India.

The general showed Dead Eye and Snowman a picture of a man whose name was Morani Tubalana. They were told that he had to be eliminated because he was a serious threat to national security.

The two were told that Tubalana was working on a weapon, which if completed and used, could kill thousands of people. Tubalana must be stopped; otherwise it could mean certain death for innocent lives.

The team was also told that Tubalana would be heavily guarded, that one slip up would spell death for the two men. The general told them that their departure would occur two days later and that they had seven days to complete their mission. This would give the sniper team the necessary time to get into location, wait for Tubalana, and get home safely, an idea that sounded good to both men.

They were each given a map of the area of operation: the exact location of the drop-off point, the location where Tubalana would be, and the exact location of the extraction point which was going to be a daytime extraction. They were warned that if they were not at the extraction point in time that they would be left.

Sniper Team Twelve understood their orders perfectly and began to prepare for the mission. Dead Eye's main weapon was a Remington Model 700 BDL 30.06 bolt action rifle that was customized for a left hander. It had a Leopold Scope mounted on it and a camouflaged synthetic stock. His sidearm was a Heckler& Koch .45 caliber pistol with an attachable silencer, if needed. Snowman's main weapon was a .308 F&N Scar rifle with a black synthetic stock and the same Leopold Scope mounted on it. His sidearm was the same as Dead Eye's, a Heckler& Koch .45 caliber pistol with the attachable silencer.

On June fourth Sniper Team Twelve was on their way to southern India. They would be dropped off twenty miles from any village, so as not to attract attention.

Dead Eye and Snowman were going over their mission again while on the helicopter. They cleaned their rifles and made one last equipment check. At 9:00 A.M. Indian time Sniper Team Twelve landed, and very quickly got into the jungle, so the chopper could get out quickly. They began their long trek across the rugged terrain.

Their first mission began smoothly and Snowman took out his map to get their bearings. Day one came to a close. The team had traveled four miles. The night passed with no incursions from any enemy patrols. The team got a good night's sleep.

They started off early to make good time. As they were walking they came upon a small swamp. They decided that it was of no danger to go through the swamp, going around would have taken too much valuable time.

Just as they began to cross, an enemy patrol was spotted by Dead Eye coming towards the swamp. The fifteen man patrol was relaxed. They were not searching for anything in particular. They had no idea the team was there, but none-the-less, taking on a patrol of fifteen men with AKs was not a good idea. Dead Eye and Snowman had no choice but to go under the water. Fortunately, for them, they had waterproof containers to put their weapons into, so as not to have them exposed on the surface or ruined by the water.

The patrol stopped at the swamp and stayed a while. They apparently were at a checkpoint in the patrol area. The team exited the water on the opposite side of the brush and slipped away. The first encounter with enemy troops had been non-violent. As day two wore on the heat and bugs became an irritating aspect for the team.

"I have never experienced such hot, miserable weather in my life" Snowman said. "Did you ever stop and think that you are from Alaska Snowman," Dead Eye sarcastically said back. The two continued on for the rest of the day without any more interruptions from enemy patrols.

The night was quiet. The men slept in shifts as they had done on night one. Snowman had first watch. He would guard for two hours and Dead Eye would guard for two hours. The only noises that were being made were the bugs and an occasional animal passing. The night passed without incident.

The team was up and moving before light. It was day three. They only had four days left with twelve miles to the three-hundred yards across; going around would have taken them way too much time.

Both men held up their rifles and scanned the area with their scopes. Neither of them spotted anything suspicious, but there was still very good reason to be cautious.

Dead Eye motioned to his partner to fall in behind him. He started crawling out into the field and Snowman followed behind. Nothing happened until they were about halfway through the field. They both heard movement about twenty yards to their right. The team took out their pistols and froze. The noise seemed to be getting closer. They pointed their weapons in the direction of the noise and waited. As the object cleared the brush, they realized it was only a deer that they had spooked while crawling through the field. They continued on and made it safely to the other side of the field and the relative safety of the jungle.

The team continued on until dark. They had traveled now another four miles. They could reach the compound, right on schedule, if they kept up their current pace. Day three came to a close and the sniper team settled in for the night. This time Dead Eye had the first watch.

While Dead Eye was scanning he heard movement behind him. He woke Snowman and they both turned slowly toward the position of the noise.

"It cannot be a sniper, or at least not a good one, to make that much noise," Dead Eye thought to himself. "A patrol might be walking right past the team, but Dead Eye would have heard them coming long before now," Snowman said to himself.

Both sniper and spotter alike pulled out their pistols, screwed the silencers on them and pointed them in the direction of the bush. They both at once unloaded their clips into the bush. They heard a scream. A wild boar fell out from behind the bush. The two settled down and Dead Eye went back to scanning and Snowman to sleeping. There were no more scares on night three.

Once again the two were up and moving again early in the morning. It was now day number four, only one more day of travel to get to the target area.

This would leave them with this one day of travel, one day of waiting for Tubalana to arrive, and a day and a half to get to the extract point. The team would have to travel four miles today and four miles tomorrow.

As they were walking they heard voices directly in front of them. They dropped to the ground and pulled out their pistols. It was a patrol of four men heading straight for the team. Dead Eye nodded at his spotter to fire. They waited until the patrol was within ten yards of them and then fired.

Completely caught off guard the men had no time to react and were taken out without getting off a single shot from their own weapons. After the team waited a few moments to see if any other enemy troops might appear, but none did; they began to move again.

Darkness began to cover the land and the team decided to rest for the night. They had traveled their desired distance of four miles. Snowman took out his map to see exactly where they were. Night number four was a quiet, peaceful night for the team.

They were up early as usual and were heading for the camp. Day number five began with no alarms or hold ups. The team needed to travel the four miles today or become behind in their schedule, and be in danger of failing, and possibly left behind.

They came upon some very thick brush that would impede their movement. They made it through the thick brush and continued to move. At about 3:00 p.m. that afternoon the team came to within sight of the camp. They went from a walk to a crawl, to make their way closer without being detected.

They watched the activities of the camp and scouted the area. Snowman counted three guard towers and six patrols. The team set up just inside the tree line that overlooked the drive way in which Tubalana would arrive. Now it was the waiting game. During the night the team slept only a little, so they could be at full potential the next day.

There was a real reason to worry, when a patrol of six men were checking the area. The guard nearly stepped right on top of Snowman, but stopped at the last minute. If he had taken one more step, the team would have been captured, tortured, and killed. They waited till the guard was a safe distance away before either made a move. The team went undetected all night.

As daylight broke on day number six, Dead Eye and Snowman were ready for Tubalana's arrival. Dead Eye's first real target would be three-hundred yards away. As the final calculations for the wind and elevation were being made by the spotter, Dead Eye noticed excitement in the camp. The guards began to form up as if someone important was coming into the camp.

There was a five car caravan that came into view and pulled into the camp. When the cars stopped four armed men got out of four of the cars. The fifth car, only three men got out at first.

"The fourth person in the car must be important" Snowman thought to himself; as one of the guards opened the last door of the car a man wearing a suit and top hat stepped out.

"This had to be Tubalana for sure," Dead Eye thought. When the man turned both of the team members immediately knew it was Tubalana. Dead Eye settled and adjusted the scope to the final calculations. As Tubalana was walking across the courtyard, Dead Eye fixed his scope on the target's chest. The sniper squeezed the trigger. A shot rang out and Tubalana fell dead, shot through the heart.

Immediately the whole camp was in an uproar. The guards began to fire their weapons frantically in every direction. The team packed up and started moving in the direction of the extraction point as quickly as they could.

Once the team was about a mile out they began to run through the jungle to the extraction point. As they were running they could hear dogs that the hunting party was using to hunt the team down quicker. The team ran till dark and only took a half-an-hour break to rest. They kept moving. Night number six consisted of mainly moving. If they did not keep moving, they would be captured or left behind for sure. The searching parties could be heard in the distance, intent on finding their leader's killer.

Day number seven broke and the team was less than a quarter mile away from the extraction point. They had thirty minutes to get there and were going to have to run the whole way. The sniper team made it to the extraction point on time. The helicopter could be seen by the team and as soon as the chopper landed Dead Eye and Snowman jumped on board. Sniper Team Twelve's first mission was a complete success.

News of Sniper Team Twelve's success reached high command and both men were rewarded. Their rest would end sooner than they expected. Due to their success, they were at the top of the list to go and eliminate targets. This time though there would be an even greater danger of not coming back alive.

3: Ukraine

Dead Eye and Snowman were in the barracks when the messenger came to them with a note from high command. The note read, “Sniper Team Twelve report to General Link’s office in one hour”. They both got ready and reported for the mission briefing.

The general showed the team a picture of a man named Yuri Bovic (last name pronounced Bovich). Bovic, the general told the team, was a major arms smuggler that must be stopped immediately. He was not only smuggling small but also large missiles and bombs.

General Link told Dead Eye that his shot, this time, would come at night. He also told the team that Bovic would be more heavily guarded than Tubalana was.

When the general handed the two their maps the name at the top read Ukraine, this is where Bovic had his large compound. The map showed the exact details of where the team would be dropped off; the location of the compound, and the extraction point, which again would be during the day. There was one very important detail on the map about the compound; the only entrance was on the south side. Once the team arrived at the compound they would have to make their way around to the south side, then wait for Bovic's arrival.

Bovic would be arriving to check on the compound to make sure that the operation was on schedule. He would arrive at night in a dark S.U.V. The only opportunity to take a shot would be immediately after he exited the vehicle. He would be surrounded by at least four body guards. The team was told, "the kill shot would be a difficult one."

Sniper Team Twelve was told that they would be leaving before light, and to report to the airfield by 5:00 a.m. in the morning. The team went back to the barracks to get their gear ready. Once they made sure everything was ready, they got some rest.

At 5:00 a.m. the next morning they were taking off for the Ukraine. The estimated drop off time was 10:00 a.m. The team would have nine days to complete the mission. They would arrive on the twenty-third of July and have till second of August to complete their mission.

Snowman figured out their time of travel. They would have six days of travel to the compound, one day of waiting for Bovic to arrive, and two days to get to the extraction point.

While in the air the team double checked their equipment one last time before their drop off, which now was only thirty minutes away. As Dead Eye was studying the map the pilot yelled, "Sniper Twelve out". The team got up and waited for the chopper to land. As soon as the chopper was on the ground the team was off heading toward the trees. The chopper took no ground fire as it was lifting off, a very good sign that they were not spotted.

Dead Eye and Snowman quietly walked through the thick forest. They had fourteen miles to get to the compound. Right off the start there was a hold up. A patrol of twenty to twenty-five men were walking through the woods. They were relaxed and so the team realized that they were not looking for anything in particular, a sigh of relief.

The team lay prone on the ground not making a move. They were not able to get on their gillie suites. They hoped that none of the men had spotted them. A snake slithered right over the top of Dead Eye's hand. It took all he could, not to throw it off. He had to let it go.

As the patrol got closer the team became tenser, a shootout, even with the element of surprise on the sniper team's side, was not favorable. They stopped and turned east; they were coming from the direction of the compound and must have just been on a routine patrol.

When the patrol was safely out of range the team began moving slowly. The wait had taken precious time away, but if they kept up the pace from here, they could make it on time. They traveled the rest of the day with no more disturbances or setbacks.

Night one consisted of travel, no sleep tonight. The team came up to a huge swamp. "To cross a swamp of this size during the day is dangerous let alone at night," Snowman said to Dead Eye. The team opted to play it safe and go around. As the night wore on the sounds of night were ringing in the ears of both men. Snowman whispered to Dead Eye, "Even in Alaska, we do not have noises like this at night".

At daybreak on day number two the team was twelve miles from the compound. They traveled another two miles or so and just ahead of them lay a very large hill. Dead Eye took out his map and saw that this was a series of hills that went on for a while.

"You should be use to climbing large hills, ah"? Dead Eye said to his spotter. Snowman shot back sarcastically with, "I am, but how are you going to manage?" At the top of the hill one could see for miles. Snowman took out his map and told Dead Eye, they were exactly ten miles from the compound.

After getting past the large hills it was now about 7:30 p.m. at night and the team came upon a stream. The steam flowed in the direction of the compound, so the team followed it. After following the stream for two miles it turned and flowed in another direction. The stream helped the team make up lost time.

As they continued through the woods Dead Eye spotted what appeared to be an old outpost. They both scanned the area with their scopes and slowly crawled toward the small hut. When they got close enough to see inside of the opening; they realized that it appeared to be empty. It looked as though it had been abandoned for years, due to the amount of overgrowth, and the condition of the hut itself. Nevertheless, the team still was cautious because the enemy could use this type of disguise to ambush an opponent. A sniper could also use it as bait when someone walked up to hut, and take them out from a safe location, when they come out into the open.

With nine miles to go and day two coming to a close the team was right on schedule. As night fell the team decided it was best if they got some sleep. The night went by with no disturbances. The team was able to get a good night's rest.

They were moving just as daylight broke on day three. The team was 8 miles from the target at the start of the day. Around 10:00 a.m. on day number three, Snowman heard something coming from his left. The team stopped and listened.

The noise was coming from their left. "What is it?" Snowman asked. "It sounds like engines," Dead Eye answered. To get a better look the team crested a hill and watched. There was something large moving through the trees. There was a clearing. The team saw large enemy troop carriers with twenty to thirty men a piece in them. When Snowman looked at his map there were no roads.

"Where did that come from?" Snowman asked. The two counted ten trucks and accounted for at least one or two they did not see. The noise of the trucks was heading in the direction of the camp. As the noise faded away the team went down to the tree line just at the edge of the road. The road was so well camouflaged that the map did not show it. For the amount of troops that were heading for the compound, something big must be going on.

The team continued on their long journey. As they walked the heat was becoming unbearable. The mosquitoes were relentless and there was an ever present danger of contracting a disease. Night was a welcome relief for the team, the coolness of the air and no more mosquitoes. The team had another restful night with no interruptions.

Day number four started with rain. At first there was only a light drizzle but as it continued it became a downpour. The rain was so heavy that neither man could see more than fifteen yards ahead of himself. They had to stop under a tree for a minute due to the heaviness of the rain. As soon as the rain lightened up a little they were on the move. It continued to rain until about 1:00 p.m. that afternoon. After the rain stopped the heat and humidity shot up like rockets. The only little relief the team had was shade from the trees. After traveling another two miles there was only one hour till dark. They would get in another half mile before dark.

They began to look for a good location to rest. During the night a curious animal scared Dead Eye to death and he nearly shot it. Other than the animal scare nothing else happened that night.

Day five began clear and cool. There was a breeze and the humidity was low. The cooler weather was a pleasant gift for the sniper team. Then the team heard the sound of a helicopter in the distance. They both dropped to the ground immediately and watched. As the chopper got closer the team could clearly tell it was not friendly. The chopper flew right over the team's location and as soon as it was clear they started moving. With five miles to go and a day and a half left of travel the team was right on schedule. They had no more trouble from the chopper the rest of the day. Apparently it was just on a normal fly over not looking for anything suspicious. As the day came to a close the team had walked another two miles and once again began to look for a place to rest. The night was peaceful and both men rested well.

At the beginning of day six they were only three miles away from the target area. They hoped that nothing would hold them up today.

The terrain was relatively level now and not as rugged as before. This made the walk much easier for the sniper team. When they got to within two miles of the compound, they spotted another outpost. This one was not empty. Looking inside through their scopes both men could see movement inside. It seemed to be a communications relay that was to warn the outpost, if there was any danger coming their way. There was a heavy machine gun mounted in the window that faced the team's direction. They had no choice but to go around. The two men crawled around the outpost and never alerted the occupants of their presence.

Once they were clear of the outpost the team could see a large clearing and saw armed guards patrolling. They could also see large buildings in the background. Snowman looked at his map and told Dead Eye that this was the compound. Now they would have to make their way around the compound, easier said than done. The team counted three guard towers and six patrols. They would have to be very careful to not make the wrong move or make any noise.

The team had to crawl the whole way around the compound which took the team two hours to complete. Once on the south side of the compound they found a good spot to set up and wait for Bovic's arrival. It was now dark on day number six and the team would have to hope that no patrols spotted them. The team went undetected all night.

It was now day seven for the team and tonight was the night of Bovic's arrival. During the day the team watched the activities of the compound. They could see armed guards carrying large boxes from one building to the next.

As dark began to cover the area, the team intently began to watch for the target's arrival. At about 10:00 p.m., they saw the headlights of three S.U.V.'s coming down a road. The gates opened and the vehicles pulled inside. Two of the three S.U.V.'s, emptied with four armed men a piece. They stayed close to the vehicle and were scanning the area intently. Dead Eye looked one man right in the eye with his scope. The man was totally oblivious to the fact that he was being watched. The third S.U.V. was emptied with another three men with AKs. Then one of them opened the passenger's back door and out stepped a man. Snowman looked through his scope and identified the target and gave Dead Eye the go a head.

The sniper put his scope on the only exposed part of Bovic's body, his head. He was so closely surrounded by the guards that any other shot was impossible. As Bovic was walking toward the building, Dead Eye followed with his scope, and then squeezed the trigger. A lone shot rang out and Bovic's lifeless body fell to the ground. The entire compound was in disarray. The guard towers were firing their machine guns frantically in all directions. The guards on the ground began to run and shoot into the woods.

The sniper team backed away and started eastward toward the extraction point. They had six miles to go and two days to get there. They had to double time their pace because they were being pursued by not only guards on foot, but the helicopter, and the trucks.

Day number eight, the first day of travel to the extraction point, they made it three and a half miles and would have to continue right through the night.

As day broke on the last day, day number nine, they were still running through the woods to make it and not get caught. They could hear the sound of the enemy chopper in the distance, but luckily, it did not sound like it was coming in their direction.

The two men had run for two days straight and now were only half a mile from the extraction point. As they were running, they could hear the sound of the extraction helicopter. The noise of the friendly chopper was very different from that of the enemy. Then at a clearing, the two men saw the chopper. Just as the chopper touched down, the two men jumped aboard, and were off. They took no ground fire despite the amount of men that were out looking for them. The enemy helicopter also never appeared which came as a welcome relief, to all on board.

While on the chopper Dead Eye and Snowman nodded to each other for another successful mission. They arrived back at the base safe and in one piece.

Once the general was notified that the mission was successfully completed and that Sniper Team Twelve was back safe, he went out to thank the team. They were granted two weeks of rest and relaxation, although their rest would not last two weeks. They would be called on sooner than anyone thought to carry out another mission.

4: Southern China

Only eight days into their leave Sniper Team Twelve was called upon for duty. They were told once again to report to the general's office. As the general welcomed the team in he apologized for their leave being cut short. He then asked if either of them had been to China.

The general put a picture of the target on the table in front of the team. The man's name was Ping Chang Won the general told them. He told the team that Won was a major drug lord and his operation was worldwide. He must be stopped immediately the team was told. Won would be visiting one of his drug facilities in southern China and this would be the only chance to stop him. The general also told the team this would be their longest mission yet, twelve days. He gave them each a map of the area and told them to report to the airfield by 11:30 a.m. the next day. They left the general's office and began to prepare for mission number three.

The team got a good night's rest before they left. The next day they got their gear and headed for the airfield. At 12:00 p.m. (noon) Sniper Team Twelve was on its way to China. While in the air, the team studied their maps as they always did. They had about a two hour flight to the drop off point.

As Dead Eye was watching out the window, the pilot yelled "Get ready". The team did one last equipment check before drop off time. Then the order came, "Sniper Twelve Out," the chopper landed, and the team got to the tree line as quickly as possible. As the chopper was heading back, the team was already deep into the woods.

Snowman calculated their exact days of travel. Day one through ten would be for getting to the facility, one day of waiting for the target to arrive and taking him out, and one night and a half day to get to the extraction point.

As day one wore on, the team continued through the thick woods. The trees were so close together in some places, that the team would need to go around large groups of trees, because it was too thick to get through. As the first day came to a close, the team was making good progress. The night was relatively quiet. The only noise being made was from the rustling of the bushes and leaves due to a moderate wind.

The team was up and moving early on day two. The day began hot and humid for the team. They had gotten use to this kind of heat and humidity before but it still could wear on a person. The terrain was not favorable either. There were high hills, which would not only take time, but strength away from the team. The hills went on for about a mile or so when Snowman checked his map. The team continued to trek up and down, and up and down the hills.

As darkness covered the land, the team settled in a little valley between two hills. This night would not be quiet like the last. As Dead Eye was on watch something caught his attention. He woke Snowman and signaled toward the trees.

Snowman, using his hands, asked what he saw. Dead Eye just pointed in the direction of the movement. Both got down behind a fallen tree and un-holstered their pistols and waited. Then, movement to the team's left.

"This is no sniper" Dead Eye thought to himself, as they waited and watched as a figure stepped out of the bushes. They still could not figure out what it was but they did know; it was not human. Then it came into view, it was a curious deer that wanted to see who the team was. The two looked at each other. Snowman took a rock and threw it at the deer to scare it away.

As day three broke, rains came with it. A steady downpour continued all day. The weather did not slow down the team. The team finally made their way over the hills and was now on relatively level ground.

Continuing through the woods, the team came upon a clearing. The field was about one-thousand yards across. The tall grass allowed the team to stand and not crawl through the field, although they did have to bend down quite a lot.

The rain began to get heavier as they continued through the field. The rain was turning the ground into a mud bath. Dead Eye almost slipped and fell into the mud. They finally made it through the field and were back into the tree line. The ground was a little firmer due to the trees blocking some of the rain. The rain, as previously mentioned, continued all day.

As night came the rain did not stop. It was not until the next morning did the downpours stop. Despite the rain the team got a good night's rest.

Day four opened with sun and more high temperatures. The team still had miles to go to get to the facility. They walked all day in the intense heat. The coolness of the night was a pleasant gift. The night dropped twenty to thirty degrees from daytime temperatures to night. This felt very relaxing on the worn out team. The night was quiet and tranquil. The sky was clear and there was a slight breeze. Everything was peaceful.

Day five began and finally the intense heat and humidity had broken, at least for now. The team came to a large lake that marked the halfway point of the team's journey. The team filled their canteens and purified the water with their purifying pills. Snowman told Dead Eye of a time in Alaska when he was hiking. He did not use the purifying pills that he was given.

"That was the sickest I have ever been," he said. "I thought I was going to die; it was so bad". After resting for about twenty minutes, they were up and moving again. They decided to go around the lake, so as not to attract attention. There was a small boat tied to a tree that must have been used by the patrols that were in the area. If they used the boat, and a patrol came by, they would be sitting ducks. The temptation to use the boat was great because it would save time and energy but it was not a good idea.

As they walked around the lake, the team noticed a small clearing. It was about a twenty by twenty clearing. This was clearly man made. The utmost quiet must be kept. The team got down, crawled forward, and noticed something in the middle of the clearing. It was covered with leaves and branches. Snowman edged forward with his knife, poking the ground to check for land mines. As he got closer, he noticed the object was square. Once he made it to the object, he began to very carefully uncover it. When he just about had the object uncovered, a lone patrolman was spotted by Dead Eye. He was heading for the clearing. Dead Eye quickly signaled to Snowman to freeze and stop uncovering the object. The man had not seen Snowman yet. Dead Eye was going to make sure that he was not going to see him either. He un-holstered his sidearm, screwed on the silencer, and aimed it at the man's chest. Dead Eye took careful aim and fired three shots into the man's body. He fell dead to the ground without making a sound, a close call for not only Snowman, but also the team and the mission.

Snowman uncovered the object. He realized. It was a communications relay. It had a telephone inside and a piece of paper with codes on it. This must have been the point at which any patrol would radio back to the facility. After disabling the device, the team continued toward the facility. The team was able to travel uninterrupted for the rest of the day. The night was peaceful like the last had been for the team.

Day six started and rain once again began to fall. The team put on their ponchos again and continued on. The rain ended sometime during the night.

Day seven began hot and humid again due to the rain. As the team was walking through the woods, the terrain leveled out some more and the team was able to make good timing. They would walk all day with no interruptions. Snowman took out his map at the end of the day to get their exact location. Night seven was peaceful like most of the others had been.

Day number eight the intense heat and humidity finally broke. The team came upon another field, which was almost twice as big as the last one. The grass was also taller, an added advantage for the snipers. This would allow them to walk normal and still be concealed. Not even twenty yards into the field, two rabbits that the team scared, jumped up, and ran in front of the team. It scared them both. When the team had about one-hundred yards to get to the tree line, they decided to rest for about ten minutes. After the break, the team made its way out of the field and back into the tree line. The team came upon a little two-track road, which they could tell had just been traveled, due to the freshness of the tracks in the dirt. The road headed in the direction of the facility.

The team heard the sound of an engine coming and quickly got down into a prone position, out of sight. It was not loud, like a truck engine. This was much smaller. The team waited for the unknown vehicle to come into view. As the sound grew louder, the team spotted a jeep with a machine gun mounted on it. The driver was the only one in the jeep. He sped right past the team.

As day eight came to a close, the team found themselves right where they needed to be. If they could keep up like this, they would be at the facility on schedule. As the night wore on clouds began to cover the sky. Dead Eye was on watch. He thought for sure rain was coming. Fortunately for the team, the rain never came.

Day nine, the team had one more day left. The team was up and moving early, as always. The clouds were welcome, because they blocked the sun, and kept the day cooler. There was also a very thick fog that lasted most of the day. Between the cloud cover and fog, the team had excellent cover from any possible enemy helicopter patrols that might come over head.

As the ninth day ended the team looked for a good place to sleep. As Snowman was on watch, he saw movement directly ahead of him. It looked like a lot of bodies. He woke Dead Eye and they got down. Through their scopes, they realized that it was a seventeen to twenty man patrol coming right at them. They could not fire on the patrol. They would be killed for sure, but neither could they get up and move. They decided to split up, crawl in opposite directions, and let the patrol pass between them in the middle. As they started to crawl, the voices of the men became excited.

"Had they spotted us?" Snowman thought to himself. Luckily they had not; one of the men had tripped and fallen.

The others were giving him a hard time for making so much noise, though they were not that quiet to begin with. The two men kept crawling away from each other, when they both froze, because the patrol was beginning to pass between them. One patrolman nearly stepped on Dead Eye when he stepped right in between the opening between his legs and then over them, a very close call again for Sniper Team Twelve.

The two men stayed in their positions until the patrol was clear. They then got up and slowly walked toward each other. The rest of the night went undisturbed.

Day ten, the last day of travel for the sniper team; as the sun rose up over the horizon, the team knew they were close. They started off early and would not stop until they had reached the facility. There were no patrols or outposts, which was surprising considering how close they were getting to the target area. The team noticed a large clearing ahead and three to four buildings.

They had made it to the facility just as darkness began to cover the landscape. The sniper team set up in a position that over looked the entrance to the facility. They counted only one guard post, no towers, and only one patrol.

"These guys must think that nobody knows they are here and are not worried about an attack, due to the small amount of security," Snowman thought to himself. The team waited all night for daylight to come and the arrival of Won.

Day eleven began sunny and breezy. The team was now watching closely for the target's arrival. They would not have to wait long. At about 11:30 a.m. that morning they saw two cars pull into the facility. Out of one of the cars exited four men, the other car only three men. Then one of the guards opened the passenger's back door. A man dressed in a suit got out.

"That is him" Snowman confirmed to Dead Eye. The sniper took careful aim at Won's chest and squeezed the trigger. A lone shot rang out. The lifeless body of Ping Chang Won fell to the ground. The guards began to shoot widely in all directions. The guards then set out searching for the killer of their boss.

The team headed westward at full speed to keep from getting caught. They continued all that day and into the night. They only stopped for a thirty-minute break and then were on the move again.

The last day brought rain along with it. The team had to get to the extraction point by mid-day or face being left behind to fend for themselves. They continued to run despite the rain and could hear the sound of the chopper in the distance. In a little clearing, just barley big enough for a chopper, the captain landed and the team jumped on board. They lifted off in the driving rain and headed for the base. Another successful mission carried out for Sniper Team Twelve.

When they arrived back at the base, the general personally thanked them. He also told them not to get too comfortable, because they would be needed on an upcoming mission that was right around the corner.

5: Cambodia

Just three days after returning from their southern China mission, Sniper Team Twelve was called on once again. Dead Eye and Snowman were at General Link's office at 9:00 p.m. The general told the team that they were headed for the small country of Cambodia. Cambodia, the general told the men, was a neutral country and so the utmost secrecy must be obtained.

General Link told the men that their target was a man by the name of Chim Lou Song. They were handed the most recent picture of what Song supposedly looked like. They were told that Song was a ruthless warlord, responsible for the multiple genocides of innocent people all around Cambodia and Laos. Due to the matter of absolute secrecy, this mission would also only be four days long. The team would be dropped off at night on the Vietnam side of the border, and would walk into Cambodia. They would also be extracted at night out of Vietnam. The chopper would not have to fly into Cambodian airspace at all. The general said that Song was supposed to be at one of his Cambodian hide outs, and would be leaving on the last day of the team's mission. This is when they were to take him out. Understanding their orders, the team left the general's office, and began preparing for the mission.

The team reported to the airfield at 7:30 p.m. the next day. By the time they were at their drop off location, it would be dark. They were expected to arrive at the Vietnam/Cambodian border at 9:00 p.m. Both Dead Eye and Snowman started preparing their night vision gear to be ready when they landed. Twenty minutes to drop off and the pilot yelled, "Stand by". The chopper reached the landing zone. The pilot landed the aircraft. Dead Eye was off the chopper first, followed quickly by Snowman. The thick jungle provided excellent cover for the team and the exiting chopper.

The first night consisted of walking. The team would have no sleep tonight. As they came across a large tree, Snowman noticed something on the side, as they began to go around the tree. When he got close enough, he realized that it was a booby trap. Had he not seen this, and walked another two feet, one of them would have tripped the wire. Both would have been killed instantly by an explosion of a mine attached to the side of the tree. They went around the other side of the tree and left the trap alone. If they would have disarmed it than, the one who checked the trap would have known that someone was in the area.

They walked all night long. The sun was beginning to rise on day one. The weather was nearly unbearable due to the heat and humidity. This was not like anything that the team had ever experienced before. The team continued through the thick jungle, and sometimes had to use their knives to cut through the brush.

Dead Eye spotted an old hut about forty-five yards ahead of them. The team slowly crept up to the hut. The two got on either side of the door. Dead Eye gave his spotter the go. He broke the door in, rifle at the ready. The hut was empty, but they could definitely tell that someone had been there recently. There was a small fire pit in the middle that still had some embers burning. Whoever occupied the hut must have left in a hurry. The team exited the hut and looked around to see if anyone was around. To avoid any entanglements with whoever occupied the hut, the team left the area. The day slowly began to turn into night as the sun started to set behind the mountains.

On watch, Dead Eye heard thunder in the distance. It began to rain just as the new day dawned. Putting on their ponchos the team began to walk. It was now day two of their four day mission. While climbing up one of the mountains, more like a large hill, the team noticed a hole in the side of the mountain.

"This was no animal hole" Dead Eye said to himself. Fear of it being occupied with enemy troops, the sniper team decided it best; they bypass it and leave it alone.

As they crested the mountain, Snowman scanned the area through his spotter's scope to see if there was any movement from a possible enemy patrol. After deciding it was clear, the team started down the mountain side. When they got to the bottom, they noticed that they had walked right into a swamp. They looked and found a way around the swamp.

The day began to turn to night and the team began to look for a sleeping place. Once they found one, they took their watch and sleep shifts. A good night's sleep was what the team needed and they were going to get it. The night also brought a much appreciated coolness.

On the morning of day three the weather was less than appetizing. The nice cool night had given way to the hot, humid weather. The team would have to walk all day in this weather.

"Don't ya wish that you were back in Alaska now?" Dead Eye asked Snowman sarcastically. All Snowman could do was nod and keep walking. The one good fortune they had, was there were no enemy patrols to deal with today. Even the enemy knew when it was too hot. As they were walking, they noticed a small road ahead. They slowly walked toward it, and examined the tracks to see if they were fresh. There were no signs that the road had been traveled very recently. As the sun began to set, the team saw two buildings in the distance. They had made it to Song's hide out.

The team got down and crawled the rest of the way. They could see what appeared to be the actual safe house of Song, due to the amount of guards surrounding it. The team set up facing the door from the right to get a clear shot. When Song exited the next day Dead Eye would take him out.

The night seemed like an eternity that never ended. Finally the sun began to rise above the trees. More alert now than ever, sniper and spotter alike watched the door for Song's exit. The hours past and Song had still not come out. Then after waiting till mid-afternoon the door opened and Song stepped out.

Dead Eye leveled his scope on Song's chest. He took a deep breath and slowly squeezed the trigger. "Ba-boom" the rifle went off. Chim Lou Song's body fell backwards dead. The guards began to run around like rats and fire in all directions. The team got up and backed away slowly until at a safe distance, and began to double-time it to the border. It was now 4:30 p.m.

They had till 9:00 p.m. to get to the extraction point. The team could hear the sound of jeeps in the distance; the guards were beginning their search for the killers. The team ran the rest of the day and into the night. As they crossed the border, the team could hear the friendly chopper and knew they were close. The team saw the chopper begin to land in a clearing directly ahead. Just before the chopper landed, the team hopped on board. They were off.

Mission number four was yet another complete success for Sniper Team Twelve. The two men were really beginning to make a name for themselves.

When they arrived back at the base, they were greeted by the general's orderly, who told them that General Link had a meeting to attend. The general regrets that he could not be there to greet the team. The two men unloaded their gear from the chopper and headed to the barracks. Once there they cleaned their weapons and waited for orders for their next mission.

6: Siberia

The weather began to change from fall to winter. While on a training exercise, the team received word that they were wanted at the general's office. The team packed up and headed for the general's office immediately. Once they were there the general walked in and shut the door. He told them they would be going to Siberia. "Siberian weather in the winter ought to suit you fine Snowman," the general said sarcastically.

Their target was a weapons smuggler who was dealing in nuclear technology. If these weapons fell into the wrong hands, it would mean death for thousands, and possibly millions of innocent lives. The team must eliminate this man, whose name was Yovani Gregoavic (last name pronounced Gregoavich). The general told the team that Gregoavic would be at one of his smuggling compounds in four days. The team would take him out then.

A picture of Gregoavic was handed to each of the men. Gregoavic, the general said, might have a beard now to try to conceal his identity. The compound would be in a section of woods that was secluded from any village or city. The map showed that the compound was directly in the middle of the woods. The team would enter the zone by train, have three days to complete the mission, and would be taken out by helicopter. They would be leaving today and immediately went to get ready.

Once the team was geared up, they were on the chopper, which would take them to a point, where they would catch the train, which would take them to the drop off point. The ride on the chopper was only an hour. They were off, heading for the train station. The team would have to walk one mile through the cold and snow to get there.

Reaching the train station, they took the first train that came in. The train would take them ten miles. Then, they would exit and sneak away to the designated section of woods. While on the train, the two men were quiet. The train stopped at the check point. This was the signal for the team to get off the train. Fortunately for them, they were the only two on that car. No-one saw them leave. The team stepped down into the snow. Then got down and began crawling to the tree line and out of sight. Just then, one of the patrol agents at the check point, walked around the side of the train that the sniper team was on. They laid there motionless. The agent never saw them. When they realized that he was gone the team started crawling again. The crawl to the tree line took the team three hours. Snowman checked the map. They were right where they were supposed to be.

As the day began to turn to night, the temperatures dropped to deadly lows. The team set up their pop-up tent; they were given to keep the wind off of themselves. The team also had been outfitted with the best winter gear in the world; ironically, it was based off a design from Siberia. Still, if the team had not had that tent to keep the wind off of them, the threat of freezing to death would have been a reality.

As dawn on day two broke, the team awoke and began to take down a half snow covered tent. After digging the tent out and packing it away, the team was up and moving. The team had to make sure that no part of their skin was exposed to the frigid temperatures; otherwise, frostbite would set in minutes.

The team continued on through the frigid weather and was nearing the compound. As they rounded a large tree, they noticed a building ahead. Checking the map again, Snowman confirmed this to be Gregoavic's compound. There were no patrols around but there was a guard bunker with two heavy machine guns mounted in it. The team crawled to a spot where Dead Eye could take his shot.

As darkness covered the land, the team once again set up their pop-up tent. They went completely unnoticed by the guard bunker. The team slept in intervals just in case there were any patrols that night.

The night gave way to day and the team already had taken down the tent, put it away and Dead Eye had his rifle ready. Snowman and Dead Eye both noticed increasing activity around one of the doors to the compound. The guards were lining up on each side of the walk-way. Gregoavic must be getting ready to exit the building. Dead Eye steadied himself and watched the door through his scope. The door opened and two men with automatic rifles stepped out with Gregoavic right behind them. Dead Eye got the confirmation from Snowman that this was their man. Dead Eye put the scope on Gregoavic's chest and slowly squeezed the trigger. The shot sounded and Gregoavic fell dead in the snow, face first. The two heavy machine guns from the guard bunker opened up but not in the direction of the team.

By the time they were raking that area with fire, the team was gone, and heading for the extraction point. Some of the guards began to run at the tree line firing their weapons but it was of no avail. The team ran toward the extraction point with all the energy they had. Just as the team exited the opposite tree line, the chopper was there waiting. They hopped aboard and the pilot took off.

When they got back to the warmth of the base, Dead Eye asked Snowman if the weather was cold enough for him and Snowman responded "Ah, that wasn't cold," in a sarcastic tone with a grin on his face.

While in the barracks the general came in and congratulated the team on yet another successful mission. He also told them, that their next mission was coming up. This mission would be warmer than this one had been. The general never said how warmer but the team would find out soon enough.

7: Vietnam

Four days after returning from Siberia, Sniper Team Twelve was once again called upon. While at the range, the general himself walked up and wanted to see the team in his office. Once in the general's office, the team was told, they were going to Vietnam.

This mission would be another three day one, like the previous. The general gave each man his map. Told them that this little country is probably the most hostile of all the ones they'd been to. The target's name was Tou Chie Sohn. Sohn was a major drug trafficker that must be stopped. When the general failed to produce a photo of Sohn, Dead Eye asked the general why? "We have no picture," was the response.

"How are we supposed to know who this guy is, if we do not even know what he looks like"? Snowman asked. The general said, the information about Sohn that intelligence had gathered, would hopefully be enough to identify him.

Sohn was to be in Vietnam in one of the villages, he used as a hide out. When authorities or anyone like that came around Sohn, his men would put on civilian clothes and blend right in with the villagers.

"Wouldn't someone turn him in for a reward?" Dead Eye asked. "Sohn has bribed the village by taking care of them. They say nothing. At his other village hide outs, he has used force to scare them into not saying anything," the general told him.

The general said, the two ways to identify the target was that his hut would be guarded with one man standing on the left hand side of the door. When he walked around the village or out of it, he had two bodyguards with him at all times. The team would leave immediately after they were geared up.

Once fully equipped, the team headed for the chopper, and was off by 9:30 a.m.

This would be considered day one of their three day mission. On board Snowman watched as the safety of the base faded into the distance. The pilot signaled to the men that they were over Vietnam, and would be landing in fifteen minutes. One last equipment check and the chopper landed. The team was off.

Not even two hours into their long hike, the heat and humidity began to wear on the two men. The flies were unlike anything they had experienced on any mission before.

"I'm sure glad this mission is only three days," Snowman said to his partner. Day one in Vietnam had not given the team a welcome arrival. The thick jungle was nearly impossible to get through at points and times. The sounds of the jungle in Vietnam were nothing like the team had ever heard.

After walking all day, the night came as a gift to the team. The heat and humidity lowered to a comfortable range for the team. On watch Dead Eye could only think of was, if they would be able to properly identify Sohn or not. The night was peaceful and quiet for the team.

Day two began with the temperatures and humidity rising again. There would be no relief for the team today. As they were walking, they came upon a river. Looking at his map, Snowman realized this river led right to the village hide out of Sohn.

The team followed the river from a concealed position, so as not to be seen by any patrols that might come by using the river, as a guide, like the team. As darkness settled over the jungle, all was peaceful. With only half a mile to the village, the team could rest for four to five hours. Then walk the rest of the way in the dark and set up a shooting position. After the rest, the team was up and moving to the village. A clearing came into view and then a hut. The light from the stars and moon allowed the team to see more huts. Checking the map to make sure this was the right village, the team set up for the shot the next day.

As night turned to day, the villagers began their activities. Snowman scanned every hut until he pinpointed the one with the one guard standing outside. Dead Eye zeroed in on the hut and waited for Sohn to exit. Not long into the morning, two armed men went and stood next to the hut where the one man was already standing. A man stepped out form the hut and looked around.

"This has to be Sohn," Snowman thought. As the man began to walk, the two armed men followed. All the pieces connected that this was Sohn. Dead Eye put the scope on Sohn's chest and squeezed the trigger. The shot hit Sohn square in the chest. He fell back dead. The entire village began to run around screaming and panicking. The three guards began to shoot wildly but the rounds were harmlessly off target.

The team was heading for the extraction point before the guards could organize their search party. The team had to get to the extraction point before dark. They ran the whole way until coming up on another river, much larger and stronger than the one they had seen before. The team would have to try to cross the river, if they hoped to make it to the extraction point on time. The current took the men twenty-five yards down river by the time they made it to the other side. Once out of the water, they continued their run to the extraction point.

Darkness was now only two hours away. The sound of the chopper could be heard in the distance. Nearing a clearing, the team saw the chopper landing. They hopped on board and were off. The team watched the jungle fade away. The observation tower of the base came into view. The chopper landed. The men were immediately sent to the general's office.

The general congratulated the team on another successful mission. He told them that their work had ended the drug-lord's reign on many villages in Vietnam. Sniper Team Twelve would not wait long for their next mission and were told to be ready to go as soon as called upon.

8: Russia

Only two days after returning from the jungle of Vietnam, Sniper Team Twelve was once again called upon. They were called into General Link's office and were briefed on the mission ahead of them. The team was told this time they would be going into a heavy populated environment. The general told the team, they were being sent to Stalingrad, Russia.

This was the most dangerous mission the team would have to face thus far. The city of Stalingrad offered little shooting angles and points of escape. Fortunately for the team, their target would be exiting a building that was overlooked by an abandoned building, just to the northeast. A map of Stalingrad was given to the team, which pinpointed the locations of each building, and had the safest route of escape.

The team was told that they would enter the city by train and make their way to the abandoned building. Fake I.D.s were handed to the men, just in case, they had any trouble from the authorities. Then the general put the picture of the target in Dead Eye's hands. The man's name was Sergei Ibrahanov. Ibrahanov was a corrupt political leader, which was in charge of a regime, which planned to take over the city and use it for their illegal activity.

The team was to take Ibrahanov out before he could become the leader of the city. Their chance would come when Ibrahanov exited the building, where he was to have a meeting with other officials and candidates for the office. If Ibrahanov got the power he desired, it could mean the suffering of the innocent people of Stalingrad.

Ibrahanov would have two bodyguards, the general told the team. They must take him out before it was too late. The general told the team that they would be leaving in the morning.

This was only going to be a two day mission for the team, so time was of utmost importance. This gave the team one day to enter the city, locate the abandoned building, and set up for the shot. The next day when Ibrahanov exited the building, Dead Eye would take him out. The team would make their way to a train leaving the city, which would stop at a checkpoint, where they would exit the train, and get to the extraction point in a group of trees to the east of the train.

The two men left the general's office and went to gear up. Once fully equipped, the team was taken to the train, which would take them to Stalingrad. They were scheduled to arrive in the city by late afternoon. Dead Eye and Snowman did not talk about the mission while on the train because there was other passengers. They did not want to take the chance of being compromised.

The train began to slow down because there was a checkpoint up ahead. When the train stopped two armed men searched every car looking for anything suspicious. Pretending to be asleep, the team went undisturbed. As the train began to move again, the two men "woke up" and watched the wilderness of Russia pass. Then the conductor signaled that they were about to enter Stalingrad. The team began to notice buildings and that the train was slowing down. The train stopped. The team grabbed their gear and exited.

Snowman took out his map to see where the location of the abandoned building was. The building was two blocks west. The checking of the map had attracted some unwanted attention. The team's fake I.D.s were about to come in handy.

Two officers walked up to the team and motioned to see their I.D.s. Both Dead Eye and Snowman handed their fake I.D.s to one of the officers. The officer looked at the I.D. cards and the men. After a few tense moments, the officer handed back the I.D. cards, nodded, and walked away.

The two men made their way to the abandoned building and entered through an opening in the side. Making their way to the ninth floor, they found a window that overlooked the office building, where Ibrahanov would arrive.

As darkness covered the city, the night was bustling with the night life of the people of Stalingrad. The people had no idea that they were being watched. The team slept in shifts through the night. The only scare was a rat that scurried across the floor, when disturbed by Snowman moving on his watch.

The sun rose above the buildings of the city. The team watched the doors of the office building to see Ibrahanov when he arrived. Dead Eye zeroed his scope on the doors and waited. Then four cars pulled up to the front of the building. Watching carefully, the team saw three of the four cars empty. About fifteen men entered the building. The fourth car's doors opened. Two men stepped out and went around to the passenger rear door. One of the men opened the door and a third man stepped out. Snowman positively identified the man as Ibrahanov. The two men walked into the building.

Now the team had to wait for the meeting to end and for Ibrahanov to exit the building. The team waited for nearly three hours before anyone started to exit the building. Then Ibrahanov came through the front doors with his two body guards, right behind him. Dead Eye put the scope on Ibrahanov's neck and fired. The bullet passed through his neck and exited out the other side. His body toppled down the steps to the bottom. His body guards began to frantically look around to see the killer. The team packed up and headed back down the stairs of the building to the hole in the wall they had entered the building through. Once in the alleyway, they went around back, and followed the map's route of escape. Walking briskly, so as not to attract attention by the officials, the team made their way to the train, which would take them to the designated drop off point. The team signaled that it was about to leave the city, and then hopped on board, and were leaving the city before the authorities were able to stop the train.

The team noticed that the train began to slow down due to the checkpoint. They prepared to jump off the train and run to the helicopter that would be waiting for them. As soon as the train stopped, the team jumped off and double-timed to the trees. They entered the trees and saw the chopper waiting. The two men hopped on board the chopper. The pilot took off. The team was back at the base before dark.

The general met the team at the landing area of the base to congratulate them. He told them that the elimination of Ibrahanov had spared the people of Stalingrad from a rule of terror. They were also told that there was another mission awaiting them but they would get a much needed rest before this one. Little did the team know, that it would be their last.

9: Romania, The Last Kill

After two weeks of rest and relaxation, that was much needed and appreciated, Sniper Team Twelve was once again called upon for duty.

"What number is this?" Snowman asked Dead Eye. "Eight," Dead Eye replied. "Eight missions and not a scratch, not bad for all we've been through," Snowman said back to his partner.

They reported to General Link's office as soon as possible. Once in the office, the general told the team that the target this time was a man who was the head of one of the most dangerous regimes in the world. He ruled by terror and terror alone. The man's name was Armon Pullichinko (last name pronounced

Poolichinko). A picture of the target was handed to Dead Eye and Snowman. Pullichinko would be heavily guarded and not very easy to take out. Dead Eye asked where they were being sent. A map of the area of operations that the general gave him read, Romania.

"Pullichinko had a compound in Romania that he visited often and was scheduled to be arriving there in two days," the general told the team. The team would have four days to complete the mission and were told they were leaving in the morning. Leaving the general's office the team went to gear up and prepare for leaving in the morning.

The two men were at the airfield at 7:30 a.m. the next day. The pilot lifted off. The team was on their way to Romania. The helicopter ride was rough due to bad weather but the pilot did a good job of keeping the chopper under control. Then the signal was given to the team to prepare to land, one last equipment check by the team before drop off. The chopper touched down. The team headed for the cover of the trees. The two men watched the chopper lift off and fly out of sight.

Snowman took out his map to get their bearings. The compound was due north from their current position. The team had a long walk ahead of them. They started out towards the compound, weaving through the thick of the trees. As their first day wore on, the team was moving at the scheduled pace they needed. The sun began to set behind the trees and the team looked for a place to rest for the night. They found a small depression in the ground and decided this was the best concealed position.

Dead Eye took first watch and immediately noticed something was not right. It was too quiet even for night. He got down to a prone position and scanned the area with his scope. He detected nothing on the first pass but when he went to re-scan the area, he noticed a branch moving. Staying put Dead Eye realized that they were being hunted by an enemy sniper. He decided to crawl slowly out of the depression and behind the base of a tree. He once again scanned the area with his scope and saw the sniper crawling around to get in behind the team. Once the sniper disappeared from view Dead Eye made his move.

He set up behind a fallen log that had a clear view of where the sniper would exit the brush and come into the clearing, where Dead Eye could take him out. Dead Eye noticed the enemy sniper crawl out from behind the brush and begin to raise his rifle to kill him and Snowman. As soon as the enemy sniper had fully raised his rifle Dead Eye fired. The round passed through the scope of the enemy sniper's rifle and into his eye.

Snowman immediately awoke and instantly pointed his rifle in the direction of the shot. Looking around, he did not see his partner, but did not dare shout, so as not to give away his position, just in case the shot was not Dead Eye. He then heard a noise behind him. He un-holstered his pistol and turned as quickly as he could. Put the barrel right in the face of Dead Eye.

"If you don't want me as a partner, there is another way to get rid of me," Dead Eye said sarcastically. "Where have you been and what happened?" Snowman asked. "An enemy sniper was tracking us and I took him out". The team moved to another location to rest, just in case someone heard the shot, and came looking.

The sun began to rise on day two. The team began to move toward their objective again. Coming up on a lake, the team noticed a dock and a couple of small huts on the opposite side.

"It must be a relay post to the main compound," Dead Eye told his partner. They then saw a boat come around the bend with eight men and dock at the hut's location. The men, with A.K.s slung over their backs, got out of the boat and began to unload boxes into one of the huts. The team stayed put and watched until the men got back in the boat and left. They then made their way around the short side of the lake and were back on track once again. The rest of the day continued with no more hold ups or interruptions for the team.

The darkness began to cover the landscape. The team settled down for the night. Snowman had first watch tonight and set up behind a small mound. After watching the darkness and listening to the sounds of the night for two hours, he could finally get some shut eye. He awoke Dead Eye for his shift and went to sleep. The night passed with no incidents.

Day three broke with a steady rainfall. The two men trudged through the mud that seemed to suck one's whole foot into the ground. Once underneath a tree that provided enough shelter from the rain, Snowman took out his map to see where they exactly were in comparison to Pullichinko's compound's location. They had five miles to go and had to make it before dark.

The rain began to come down heavier and heavier. It was so bad at one point that the team could not see five yards ahead of them. As they continued, they noticed through the rain, what seemed to be an outline of a building. Edging closer through the trees and rain, the team realized this was Pullichinko's compound. Looking for a good spot to set up for a shot, Dead

Eye noticed a small rise just to their right. They crawled up to the top and set up. If the intelligence was correct, Pullichinko would be leaving tomorrow. Dead Eye would take him out then.

The team counted six guard towers with heavy machine guns, and four guard bunkers with light machine guns. Due to the rain, there were no patrols for the team to worry about for now. As night came, the rain began to stop. Dead Eye noticed five men exit one of the buildings, when the rain stopped completely and begin to search the area. Fortunately for the team, the patrol never came close enough to cause a scare.

The last day of the mission opened with sunshine and a breeze. Snowman watched through his scope, the guards change shifts and more men exiting a building in front of the team. Now it was the waiting game for Pullichinko to show himself. Around 1:00 p.m. that afternoon, both Dead Eye and Snowman noticed about twenty armed men fall into formation in front of one of the buildings. Dead Eye zeroed in on the door in which the men were gathering. The door opened. A man and a woman stepped out. Snowman positively identified the man as Pullichinko. Dead Eye put the scope on Pullichinko's chest, took a deep breath and fired. The bullet struck Pullichinko in the chest killing him instantly. The woman screamed and ran for the building. The guards began to fire their weapons. All of the guard towers and bunkers also opened up with their machine guns, peppering the ground with hundreds of rounds.

The team backed down the small rise and started to run for the extraction point. The guards began to chase after them in all directions searching for the killers. The team could hear the guns and shouts of the chasing enemy guards. The team saw a clearing about fifty yards ahead, and realized that it was the extraction point, when they heard the chopper coming in to extract them.

As the chopper began to land, Dead Eye motioned to the door gunner, that they were being followed by enemy guards not far behind them. Nearing the chopper both men thought they were home free. Just then shots rang out from behind the team and Dead Eye dropped, immediately. The door gunner spotted the guard and riddled him with bullets. Dead Eye got up and began to start for the chopper again, but noticed Snowman didn't move at all. He stopped and went back to his partner's body, only to realize that the rounds from the enemy gun had struck Snowman in the back. Dead Eye yelled to see if he was alive but no response. Everything seemed to stop as Dead Eye realized his partner and best friend was dead. He came to and picked up Snowman's body, and his rifle, and ran for the chopper. He put his body on the chopper and hopped on board while the door gunner provided cover fire. The pilot lifted off just before the enemy guards could completely close in on the chopper. As they flew away, the door gunner cut down another ten to fifteen men who came into the clearing trying to shoot the chopper down.

Dead Eye leaned against the side of the chopper and began to cry. He could not believe Snowman was really dead. When they made it back to the base, Dead Eye got off the chopper and picked up his partner's lifeless body. The general came out as quickly as he could and saw Dead Eye bearing the dead body of Snowman. Two men with a stretcher ran out to get Snowman's body from Dead Eye. Dead Eye laid the body on the stretcher and saluted with tears in his eyes.

Dead Eye then went back to the chopper to get his gear as well as Snowman's. The general walked up to Dead Eye and told him that he was sorry for the loss, and that he was proud of Sniper Team Twelve for completing another mission. Dead Eye said nothing, but only saluted and walked away. While Dead Eye was in his bunk, he remembered the training and missions he had been through with Snowman.

He then began to write a letter. After he was done, he got into his dress uniform and went to see the general. Once in the general's office, he handed him the letter. The general read it and looked at Dead Eye.

"You want to be relieved of sniper duty?" he asked, in somewhat amazement. The general got quiet for a minute, then answered Dead Eye. "With the circumstance at hand, I understand a request of this sort". He then wrote Dead Eye a paper stating he was being honorably discharged from sniper duty. “Thank you sir,” Dead Eye said to the general. He then stood up, saluted to the general and walked out.

Dead Eye never went back to be a sniper. He could not bring himself to return to duty and go on another mission with someone other than his former partner, Snowman. Dead Eye kept Snowman’s .308 F&N Scar rifle to always remember his partner and best friend. He moved to a small town in Alaska and lived there for the rest of his life.

Conclusion

Sniper Team Twelve was the best in the business. Dead Eye and Snowman had completed the most dangerous missions that faced them with absolute perfection. Sniper Team Twelve's legacy in the record books remains untouched, even though, they only had eight missions. The way they completed those missions is what earned them the honor and respect that they had among other sniper teams. Sniper Team Twelve would only now exist in writing from here on out.